ALLOW ACTION TO DOMINATE

ALLOW ACTION TO DOMINATE

Dilip Kumar Ojha

KALPAZ

ISBN : 978-93-5128-036-1
Price: 140

First Published 2014

Published by

Kalpaz Publications
C-30, Satyawati Nagar,
Delhi-110052
Ph. : 9212142040
E-mail: kalpaz@hotmail.com

Laser Typesetting : Rudra Computer Graphics, Delhi
Printed at : G. Print Process, Delhi

Cataloging in Publication Data--DK
Courtesy: D.K. Agencies (P) Ltd. <docinfo@dkagencies.com>

Ojha, Dilip Kumar.
Allow action to dominate / Dilip Kumar Ojha.
p. cm.
ISBN 9789351280361

1. Self-actualization (Psychology) 2. Success. I. Title.

DDC 158.1 23

Dedication

I dedicate this book to my loving wife. She supported me in all my hard days. She made me what I am today. She also taught me to get rid of fear.
I am greatly indebted to my parents, who have acted as a catalyst in my life.

Contents

Preface

Millions of people are living in a comfort zone, and are not willing to come out from it. They just bury their master piece idea, without taking action on it. They are very reluctant to untie the rope, which is holding them. You have to come up and make an identity of your own, which is not very easy. If you are eagerly looking for it then you have to learn to detach from the past. Your success is directly proportional to your thought and what you visualize. Learn to take your steps with boldness, and push your limit, and never worry about perfection. You should never see difficulty in every decision but you should see opportunity in every decision. It is a pity that so many people just give up and accept defeat in the hands of obstacle.

Learn to step on the obstacle and go ahead and create your image. Remember you will not get a second chance in your life. See your future where you can enjoy a delightful new sense of well being. Only learning alone will not help you, try to take action. Never give space to fear. Allow action to dominate on you. Only action will help you in becoming a doer, rather than just a preacher.

Dilip Kumar Ojha

Acknowledgements

First I would like to thank my family for creating an environment, where I could write at any hour of the day. This book couldn't have been written without the help of newspapers, old books and magazines. I also thank my parents, who have acted as a back-bone in my life. I also thank myself for showing me the hidden talent of writing. Last but not the least I thank to the Almighty.

Dilip Kumar Ojha

Introduction

The bitter truth of life is in your hands to be dominated by fear or by action. If you allow fear to dominate then it will stop you everywhere and you will never come closer to success. Your mind will fabricate thousands of reasons to procrastinate your work. You will never be able to take your first step. It will completely freeze you. It may even paralyse you.

Sometimes fear may even bury your ideas. If you allow action to dominate, it will act as a jack for you and will put you on the right track. Sometimes it becomes so difficult to balance between life and work that it appears to be an impossible task.You have to come out of your vortex and start with your action habit. If you will not take action then your mind will be filled with doubt and clutter. You should never make space for doubt. Always take action and feel free to take your step. Once you achieve your small step then raise the bar and think of taking the next step. If you allow fear to dominate then your false evidence/illusion will always appear true. You must have seen the construction site of a house, in the beginning everywhere you see things lying scattered here and there, but slowly as you take action your house gets ready and everyone praises it. In the same way when you start a business in the early stage, it looks so much daunting, but slowly as you take action you get confidence in your work. If your fear is holding you, then untie your fear and start taking decision. If you have to use A.T.M for the first time then you may end up asking all details and ideas from your friends, but the moment you go inside and operate yourself, you overcome fear, the remedy of fear is action. You have to make yourself an action dominated body and an action dominated mind. Fear is nothing but our own imagination, after coming out of the A.T.M operating yourself you will laugh at yourself the way you had imagined like it might go wrong, or it might have problem. In reality it wasn't. It was a bit fun using the A.T.M. whenever you feel fear is approaching or holding you then try to confront it, you have to keep facing every time it comes and then you will see your fear dissolving. You have to deal with failure.

Sometimes you may feel like giving up but you have to continue in spite of difficulty or lack of success. There should not be confusion of fear and fate.

Fate is in your hand. You have to control your fate. Sometimes fear can be a fuel in disguise where you may need to spare some time, by jotting down your fear along with your plan and action. You do not have to risk your life because of fear. You just have to change the path which you have taken.

Unless you take risk, success will never come to you. You have to inculcate courage within you to overcome fear and take action.

Sometimes fear may be a friend, or a foe. When you allow action to dominate, you take control of your fear, and will learn to take action. Once you start practising a habit of taking action you will never end up searching for your success. The more action you take the better it gets. Whatever you are now, it is because of the visualisation you had made long time back. Your success is directly proportional to your thought and what you visualise.

You allow your mind to be dominated by action and then you see the achievement. If your mind is full of doubt with trivial matter then you may not be able to think of great ideas. You should keep a list of thought changer so that you can change your trivial thought.

2

Reduce Your Expectation

2

Reduce Your Expectation

We people have a habit of expecting more than what we do. Learn to break free your expectation. Your expectation will no doubt help you but when you do not get your expectation, then you might feel bad. Instead of expecting you should learn to give more and let others expect from you. You just stop your expectation from others and let your action decides what to do.

Try to do everything what others are expecting from you. Everyone has a unique style and potential. The more and more you compare yourself with others, your expectation level will go up. You should try to become a role model for others and let others emulate your life style.

You should learn to detach from your past and start thinking about how to be a different person in future. Many people have an insatiable curiosity to have more, but what is more important is to dream something, which is realistic. You can't just end up dreaming for everything. Just visualize your expectation which should be realistic, and see yourself. You can compare yourself to yourself. You have to present a vision of yourself and then you can achieve it.

You should never under price or overprice yourself from others point of view. You should be internally controlled and should not be dependent on other's judgement. Our expectation is so high that sometimes we just forget that it is not our look or our costume.

It is a matter of connection of the souls, which we have visualized. Instead of expecting what to be, you should visualize what you want to be and never allow vision to get down of the track. Our expectation level should be moderate and reasonable or else we will get disappointed very often.

Expectation is more or less an anticipation for something. If it is realistic or balanced, then your expectation does not disappoint you, or else you will have a sinking feeling of sadness. It is natural to have an expectation, but what is more important is, you can control your expectation and not others expectation.

There is no harm in reducing your expectation from others and learn to do more. If your expectation is too high and suppose you do not get, then you will get shattered, but if your expectation is a moderate one, then you can learn from your failure. Fear of failure will make you strong.

If you really learn to reduce expectation, then you will come closer to your happiness. It doesn't mean you shouldn't have high expectation but you should be ready to face disappointment and hatred in yourself.

Learn to take action on your realistic expectation. You should set a reasonable goal. Sometimes people believe that having a big expectation can bring a big miracle. You will get happiness, when you will not expect anything from others. You will feel more happy and content.

3

Be A Doer

You must inculcate a habit of implementing rather than just thinking about it. If you have any ideas reeling in your mind, and if you are not taking action, then your ideas will fade and might become weak. There is no perfect time to start, suppose you have a new car and you are scared of driving. At times you feel that others may hit your car in the week days and you are planning to take out on Saturday and Sunday then suddenly it strikes that normally on Saturday and Sunday freshers practice.

You will end up postponing unless you take action.

You have to make your own weather and never wait for the perfect time to come. You have to take action because sometimes we feel, that we have no initiative. You have to act independently and should never wait for others to push you or tell you to start.

No doubt it is really difficult to balance your work but you have to do it. You have to concentrate on one thing before taking up another. You should never accumulate all your work and wait for the right time to start. You should be true to yourself and never be externally controlled and must answer to yourself rather than answering to others, develop a habit of validating internally rather than external validation. Just practice to say how can I do it instead of saying, I can't do it. When you say how I can do it, you put your mind to work and create a positive attitude, when you say how can I do it your mind will get confused and will stop working.

You have to do and for that stop accepting whatever fate brings.

You cannot change the outside world. It is you who have to change and use your ideas to adjust and prosper, you should never hesitate to make mistake. If you are busy making mistake a day will come, and you will become superior without mistakes. Many people feel inferior, but what is more important is, a certain flaw may not be a good reason to label you as an inferior. Come out from that sinking feeling, start doing instead of burying your precious ideas.

If you feel that you do not have a gut to take action, then with a small amount of initial discipline, you can create a new habit of taking action. You have to keep commemorating your action habit, or else you may forget. You have to develop taking action and stick to it. You have to enjoy while doing it. If any negative feedback comes then keep a list of thought changer which can change your negative into a positive one.

Just do it and be a doer you shouldn't get discouraged or allow any slightest feeling of giving up.

4

Be A Self Starter

You should be a self starter. It is not possible for anyone to hire somebody for you to guide you every time you go wrong. You have to become that somebody and take the proper steps. If you are a self starter you can handle any situation and for that you have to make your mind very acute. You must be quick enough to interpret, analyse and understand. To be a self starter you have to be a keen observer.

Allow your brain to take action you should give some time to make your brain sharp by allowing your brain to actively participate in most of the activities you do.

Suppose if you are not able to think wherever a little bit of resonable amount of thinking is needed that means you are dull, less sensitive and less observant. You have to change your way of thinking. You have to cover all aspect, think from all angles and come to the best conclusion. You should come up with creative ideas and always allow new information to get inside. You must never cut off from your friends and stay isolated. You should mingle with everyone and try to get good ideas from everyone and try to assimilate them with what you have. To be a self starter you can go for a pep talk and focus yourself as somebody who does his work on his own. You have to be ready to accept even those work which may not be comfortable to you. Slowly you will realise that you can handle all new work. Slowly you will get accustomed to discomfort. If you really want to be a self starter you should be ready to catch the opportunity and should be ready to tackle and shoot out problems without being told or reminded. You maintain your self-esteem and never hesitate to contribute your precious ideas.

Always develop a habit of taking a new project on your own initiative without others help. You have to become energetic and vibrant and stop taking help from seniors frequently.

You should always be on the lookout for new ideas and create an ability to think differently, suppose your mind stops working out for new ideas then just relax your mind and your ideas will start flowing then later on, you can segregate them. Suppose you have a tree and you know after some year you will get fruits. Suppose if you will not use or give them they will get rotten. In the same way thousand of new ideas keep fluctuating in our brain. If you keep your ideas accumulating or storing then the ideas will get rotten and will be of no use. You have to implement it. Being a self starter you should never bury your ideas. You should be ready to take out new ideas and act upon it, and must execute your ideas.

You should always encourage your brain to be innovative in order to be a self starter.

5

Evolution of Thinking

Gradual development of thinking will put you on the right track. First of all you should find out the type of people you are interacting or the places you are selecting for an outing. You can't do big things, if you keep yourself engaged with trivial matters. If you really want to come up then you have to think differently and learn to do a lot of whatever you are doing. It will pave your chances of success. Even if you fail, try to find out fuel in the failure, try to take feedback in a positive way. If you will focus your attention on negativity and scarcity then you are going to experience the same thing.

You should learn to count your blessing, if you practice it on a fairly regular basis, then you will benefit more than you can imagine.

Make use of your creative mind and come out of the comfort zone.

If you know you are doing the right thing then just relax and perform.

Try to think differently, when everyone else thinks alike you should keep yourself apart from the crowd. You must have an insatiable curiousity to change your thinking. If you think that you do not have enough money then you continue to have that feeling.

If you focus on abundance then you will have more money. You should look out for new ideas and new methods to change your thinking. If you feel a mutual gain is possible then allow yourself to get connected with bright people, sometimes boredom will help you to come out from your mundane life, it leads to creative thinking and fresh thought. To change your way of thinking, you have to come out and be a cosmopolitan. Living with different culture is perhaps the best way to change your way of thinking, you have to understand others culture and way of thinking. You will develop a broad tolerance and then you will learn to adjust. You are a product of your information. Find out the right information source and change your life, find out the people you are interacting, everyone has a different perspective.

You have to change your perspective and rethink about it. Try to associate with those people who talk about prosperity and have a winner edge. Try to come out from the comfort zone and try something new. Life is difficult and full of challenges and what is more important is the attitude we choose to perceive these challenges and the mentality we choose to perceive these challenges.

Sometimes great ideas which affect our attitude in a positive or constructive manner impinge on our daily life sometimes directly, dramatically and sometimes subtly. They are influential in shaping the quality of life. We normally show reluctance and say "that's it or I have got it" Merely saying I have got it will not help you. If you take it honestly then there is a need of constant reinforcement by reading again and again or by listening to tapes or by associating with people you can grow with. It has to be internalised through the constant reinforcement, you can even discuss positive ideas and thoughts with your friends no matter whether they accept it or ignore it. When you discuss, you reinforce it and it gets internalised, and then you see yourself the attitude you have inculcated and soon you will see that your life is rewarding.

6

6

Gracefully 'No' with Self-Discipline

Suppose you go to your friend's party and over there if they insist you to have alcohol and if you really want to say no then you can say gracefully no to them. Just tell them you do not feel like it and you are not a drinker but a thinker. Tell them that you are too cool for that stuff and you can also add that you have an allergic to alcohol.

You can say that you do not drink on days that end with 'Y'.

You have to be strong and stand for something. You can say no to friends, to drugs and to adultery.

If you have a quality of grace then you can handle beautifully and gracefully 'No' in a peaceful manner. You do not always have to agree. You have to be strong enough to say no to life's many temptation from illicit sex to adultery, it will help you to stay on track and achieve your health goals.

Suppose if you are being offered alcohol and if you say I can't it means you are forcing yourself to do something you do not want to do.

If you say I do not, that means you have a control over the situation that will help you to break your bad habits. That time is an acid test for you whether to say no or yes, it tests some aspect of your character. Sometimes it becomes so difficult to resist but with a little practice of tough love and self control you can do it. Do not put yourself in a place to be tempted. If you are struggling with alcohol do not go or keep alcohol at home.

Self discipline will help you to overcome temptation and will create a new habit of thought and action. There should be a will power.

The time has come to emphasize the need to develop how you think. You try to push yourself beyond your fear. You should be ready for difficult sacrifices.

7

Five Tips for Leadership Qualities

1. Disciplined Mind

To have a disciplined mind you have to undergo rigorous training.

You can't do it in a day or two. Everything comes under play like school, college, training and post graduate courses but you can even do it without even joining. Just take a look at some of the big names and try to find out their background and you will see most of them have not even done their formal education. You can learn from nature, from your parents and by interacting with prosperous people. Instead of setting a goal, deadline, plan and action you see your strength and ask yourself the resources you have and what can be created. It is better to avoid collecting ideas of others and resituating it.

You should have the gut to say no to other ideas and concept. You can repudiate their logic and workout on your own ideas and try to explode your thinking. Make friendship with nature and try to understand the real world. Whatever tools you pick up may be insufficient to be a good leader. You have to work on it pragmatically.

2. Amalgamate and Unify

You have to learn to integrate the different sources of information. You have to learn to balance between your work and life you have to check your workshop and the workers whom you are going to assign the work, accordingly you have to give flexible support to your workers. Fine words and intentions deliver nothing unless you act on it and highlight the priorities. You have to synthesise strategic team development, successive planning and management development. You must feel a thrill of challenge, and check your ideas which are practical. You have to mix and amalgamate the strategy of completing your work no matter whether others are giving a helping hand or not you have to unify yourself and find out your strength and weakness, there should be an amalgamation of body, brain and environment to be a good leader. Whenever you think something new, actually is an old idea. You just have to associate it and practice on a fairly regular basis.

3. Innovative

Time has come to think innovatively to stay success and competitive.You have to generate new ideas. Only ideas alone will not help you. It has to be evaluated and implemented. Innovation will keep business competitive you should innovate your ideas rather than reacting to the innovations of others. The tools of innovation are ideas which are the raw materials. You have to assimilate your ideas, and if required segregate some of them. You shouldn't keep shuffling your ideas and allow it to stay and then see the changes. You have to build your self esteem and believe that you have innovative ideas. Do not try to listen to feedback, when you are in process, when your ideas are clear like a crystal then you can take others feedback. You shouldn't allow criticism to stifle your innovative ideas.

Your ideas will come to you only when you will not strive to think, keep your mind open and relax then creative ideas will flow.

4. Empathise Others

This is a great quality of a leader. You must have ability to understand others feeling and emotion. You should try to absorb others feeling and for that you have to put your legs in their shoes and think from their point of view. At times you do not have to say in words. Your body language and gesture convey the message. You can sometimes paraphrase their statement. But at the time of taking decision you have to take an objective decision. Being a leader you will have to talk to your workers and understand but what is more important, you should know when to turn it on and off. You must know when to control your emotion. It you are empathetic then it should be at your will and you should know how to get connected and disconnected at your own will. It will be easier for you to interact and take proper decision.

Sometimes in an organisation some decision and actions are deemed unfair or unjust, and in turn the affected employee experience feeling of anger, outrage and resentment. Then conflict starts a cold war and a will for revenge.

At this point the baseless argument, unfair dialogue and unhealthy criticism takes place. To manage adverse situation and to avoid conflict empathy must be practiced. There are some managers who comfort employees in a tense situation, get to the source of problem, but do not get emotionally involved. Empathy is difficult because it needs emotional control, understanding and acceptance of how someone feels and an objective evaluation of the situation.

5. Self Reliant

You need to become a self reliant. It is not possible to hire somebody to check your every actions. We shouldn't expect others to help. If you are self reliant then it will free you from difficulties. You can formulate and clarify vision, you can take out potentials of your workers. You have to act as a helping agent. It means you have to be a catalyst in sparking the interest in them. The focus shouldn't be only on yourself but the changes you can bring in others. True leaders take more than their share of the blame and less than your share of the credit.

The onus is on you. You should step up and take full responsibility for wrong decision. You should never play blame game. Leaders do not push it off. You should point at yourself. As a leader you should give the credit and take the blame, you should pass on kudos you receive from your seniors to the deserving individual. If you are one trick pony then you cannot be a jack of all trade, when something goes real good you should say, you did it.

A leader is known not for his own potential and capabilities but the ability he has to bring out the best in others. True leader do not have a habit of saying I instead of I they say we. There is no I for them when they talk about their team normally leader use I when accepting responsibility for failures. They promptly use we when comes success. You should focus on the solution instead of focussing on the problem. The bitter truth of a leader is if he wants to bring changes then he will have to face. You have to be practical and select a language of the visionary. Language is the reflection of yourself.

If any subordinate says that your language is too poor to express the best thought for a project then he shouldn't be underestimated. Success comes before work only in dictionary but in reality work comes before success. True leaders should radiate the positive feeling.

8

Risk Taking

Doing interesting things always includes an element of risk. The real living is out in the open. Normally we people look for a govt. job only to be secured, it is just an illusion. If you really want to live a satisfying life you should take risk, never fear of the obstacle and come out of the comfort zone. The very nature of life requires risk taking. You should create your own path rather than making a good resume to get a good job. You have to select your path and do not follow the path taken by the masses. You can follow the path of success. The more and more you elude yourself from taking risk then you will never achieve anything. You cannot discover a new life without detaching from your past. The person who risks nothing, does nothing, fear of failure is so deeply rooted that they can't anticipate anything other than loss. They never think about the possibility of success. All successful people do things in a different way. They never hesitate to take calculated risk. Failure is not a big loss in the long run but the benefit you are going to accrue, if you get success will be much more than the pain of failure which is temporary but the pain of regret for not taking the risk will become permanent. Either you will become successful or might become the master of excuses. Visualize yourself in future and then decide what to do in present.

No one has become successful without following the recipe of the great people. Successful people will like to push you up, they will be honest and straight forward with you. You should take action, even if you do not get the satisfaction, by doing this you will come closer to your success, you should learn to unlearn and keep abreast all the current information and then take actions, something has to be given up to move forward. When you are not happy with where you are you should be willing to take risk. Only by taking risk you are likely to succeed, you should try new things that you have always wanted to try but were too scared. You should take the chance that could bring you what you want in life or else it will haunt you in your future.

9

How to Untie Your Rope

Sometimes it so happens that even if you want to do something, something holds you back, it may be your mood to start or the fear of others reaction. Just start and take the challenge. If you keep waiting for your good mood then you will have to wait endless numbers of hours to start your work. First of all there is no mood factor, it is your way of thinking, suppose you are being chased by a dacoit, then will you say at that time that you are not in a mood to run. At that time the word mood will not come to you.

In the same way, when you do not want to recall the word mood for such cases, then why to give so much importance at the time of taking challenges and action.

At times you get worried about what others might be thinking of you. In case you fail then what would be their reaction. If you keep worrying about others then you cannot push yourself on the right track. Many people have been brought up in such a way that fear of criticism is deeply rooted in their mind. They never come out from the comfort zone, it is the time to pause and reflect. You should never follow the majority.

Majority of them are not happy and do not know the real meaning of success. If you follow the successful people you will see yourself, they do what majority are not doing, they take a different path and are always ready to face criticism and later on they become the public figure and centre of attraction for the majority.

When I was writing my first book "Roll up your sleeves and say bye to burn out." I was overwhelmed by the size of the work and the pressure was mounting on me. Then I braced myself and exerted all my pressure and started writing in baby steps.

I mean to say you shouldn't procrastinate and put off for the next hour. If you really want to change your life you have to untie. We are very reluctant to do something different, it might be the fear of failure, fear of risk or lack of ideas. You should never worry about perfection. You know an object at rest tends to remain at rest. You have to read good books and stay motivated. You must say how to do it and practice saying when other people can do then why can't I do it. You can get success in life.

10

Learn to be Above Average

If you really want to succeed in life, then you have to be above average. For that you have to stay focussed and take responsibility of your action. You should be ready to admit if you make a mistake. Whatever act you do to make up for the loss that you have made is your antonement. A weak desire to succeed in life will not help you. For that you must have a strong desire. Half hearted effort doesn't produce half results. It produces no result. You should do everything as quickly and effectively as you can, you should always look for new opportunities. Your life will not give you chance to prove yourself again. You should try to associate with successful people. If you keep thinking to do something different then you will never be able to do.

If you really want to get noticed in the crowd,then you will have to do something different. You should start thinking like a successful people.

You should never indulge in trivial matter, think like an above average person. You should look at the life of successful people and try to emulate them, you shouldn't discuss about people and things. Whenever you have time go for ideas and discuss about ideas. Whatever steps you take, it should come out from your heart and not from the mind. Whatever you wish to have or you wish to do and you are not visualising it through your heart then your wish will not come true. Always look for things to get your thinking process triggered. If anything raises the curiosity you should write down so that it will stimulate your thinking. You should be ready to embrace change, uncertainty and doubt. Always ask yourself how to think instead of what to think. You should create the ability to connect between two separate things which do not have any resemblances. You should prepare for positive and allow new things to enter. You should learn to live fearlessly and achieve success. Learn to build a strong relationship with yourself and just do something different.

11

A Responsible Life

1. You are responsible for the choice of your friendship.
2. You are responsible for what you do about your feelings and emotions.
3. You are responsible for your life and well being.
4. You are responsible for your happiness.
5. You are responsible for your beliefs and values.
6. You are responsible for the level of consciousness.
7. You are responsible for your choice, decision and action.
8. You are responsible for the fulfilment of your desire.

If you want to be a responsible person and want to do something different you have to allow action to dominate your mind, you have to perform your work and get the result, you have to be result oriented.

Always remember your responsibility even if no one is watching you. Your responsibility is to have a clear vision of what you want to do.

Your responsibility is to be a leader and not a follower, you have to make a path for the others to follow even if the path is not safe. No one can live life for you. Whatever is happening is the result of choices you make or have made.

Either you will take the responsibility or you will play the blame game. You will blame your father, mother, your friends and finally the whole world. When you want to blame others for not getting success it is better to ask yourself, how can I help myself, you have to be ready for the opportunity and must become the right person for whatever opportunity is right in front of you.

In order to know your responsibility, you have to hang around with your friends who are responsible, and must rethink once again to get success in life. The world is not going to change, you will have to mould yourself in the responsibility you take, and the thoughts that comes to you.

Try to check yourself what you are doing, how you are spending and wasting your time. No doubt everyone wants to succeed in life and wants to live a prosperous life. To speak with you honestly, just tell me are you really serious about your dream and desire to succeed. If you are waiting success to come and knock, then just forget it you have to be a responsible person to win in life.

Some people feel that success is inborn, ingrained and innate it may be true for some people who may be rich.

Hereditarily,if you think that way, then you may never consider your responsibility seriously and for you, there may be no such word as opportunity in the dictionary.You must take responsible steps and never expect defeat in the first place, and in case you fail just step on it and go ahead.

Try to be responsible at home and at office, and for that you have to emulate others who are more responsible and successful, talk like they talk, think like they think. You must have come across many people who have a big tummy and keep asking, how to reduce. Even if you tell them the basic exercises, I don't think they will do, for that they should have a burning desire.

If you are a professional boy then you may like to go to college everyday and may love to pile up degree and when time comes to decide your goal or future then you would fall sick, and sometimes you may not like to talk about job or career.

Slowly you will become a backbenchers of the class and may lose your interest in studies I mean to say you do not have to keep adding your degree to become successful just try to take action differently, and never settle with what your friends have settled with.

Let them think, what they think of you, just do it and prove yourself that you can do it and for all these you must have a burning desire and a good and broad vision of what you are doing. Others may not know but your visualisation should be clear.

12

Behave Like A Rich Person To Be Treated Like One

Some people have a plebian sense of dress, the way they put on dresses seems so bad that they will never get respect from the common people. If you want others to respect, then never think that you are low in front of them and never accept the limitations which are self imposed, never bow and apologize for simple request. If we belief we are bound for a particular destination for big things then our belief and vision will radiate outward.

This energy will force other people around you to respect you. No doubt you are trying to act but it is up to you to make in real, just act as if you are worthy of respect.

You should never under-price yourself,your price tag should be high.

Mingle with successful people and keep distance from the pessimist, and then they will know about your strength and greatness, and if you can, invite them on your son's birthday or on some house warming ceremony. By doing this you will come closer to them and slowly your thought will start changing and a day will come, when both of you will become equal. All those who had criticise you earlier will now come to you with eulogy and start respecting you for your confidence and then by following this, will eventually lead to a successful life.

Just act as if your every move is creditable, and you disserve to be respected from others. Do not wait for others to come and tell you, that you deserve respect. You start acting from now that you are not an ordinary person.

Everything is created twice, first you have to visualize and then you will get, suppose you have a purse and you hardly keep 200 rupees or 400 rupees then your visualisation knows to maintain that level in your purse. Now try to keep more than 2000 rupees and less than 5000 rupees then you will see yourself that even after 2 months you have somewhat more or less the same amount. You don't have to doubt about it just try one time, and you will see yourself the power of visualization. You must feel that you have what you wish and then visualize it everyday and never underestimate its power.

13

Maintain Distance and Never Disclose Everything

You are right if you are not hesitating to tell about your plan and feelings to others, but it is better to avoid. It will help you in your long run. If you keeping talking about your plan then you will become an object of derision, if you will talk too much with somebody then he may take you to be a common man and you may lose respect. Do not share your real ideas to everyone, learn to intimidate fear in others by speaking less and make them hollow. You will get more respect. Whenever you speak with your subordinate let them start first and when you speak do not be in a hurry to reveal every thing. Your brief answers will help you to get more respect, or you may end up raging something rubbish, or you may spoil your own nest. Once the words are out, you cannot take them back. Words are the tools of your thinking. A single word may create respect or disrespect. Suppose you have some ideas then speak a little about it and let others talk about it. Always be ready to listen to their feedback.

Your appearance and sense of dressing should speak more than words, but if your body language is not good, then there will be a leakage of your personality, and your friends will take it for reality, words are power, they vibrate. So speaking too much dilutes the power within.

When a child babbles, it is accepted, but if you babble all the time you will lose your respect. Try to maintain some distance, I mean it is good to mingle, but at the same time if you do not keep distance you will not get respect. Try to develop values within you and become a man of values it will instil fear in others and you will get respect. You do not have to ride roughshod on them or act like a dogmatic, if you want others to respect then speak less than necessary and maintain some distance and never behave like a common man. You should give a rank to yourself and focus on the dresses you put on.

14

Recreate Your Image

You have to come out and take control of your appearance and emotions. You have to mould yourself in such a way, that commands attention, and be the master of your own image and do something different that will make you outstanding.

Time can never be altered, if you want to succeed, then learn to adjust the situations as they come by. Come out from your stubbornness and let yourself flow with the nature and allow the same freedom to your subordinate. You must never doubt your ability to win, and in case you meet with a temporary setback, you should become more determined to succeed. Learn to say "I am success;" instead of saying "I will be successful". Try to succeed first in your inward inner self and then slowly it will be translated into your outward life. Learn to differentiate yourself from others, and develop loyalty from others. Remember inculcate a habit of positive thinking. It will motivate you to do the other things required. For this you must have a sound body and mind. Exercise is important for everyone, he or she should work out. This is the age of multitasking, everyone has bowed under the pressure of performing well. Follow single task. Try to do something you have never done. You never know, when there will be a life changing impact on you. You can even change your brain by simply doing some aerobic exercises, that will help you to think more positively, and will help you to grow more resilient. You have to make a positive self image because it exhibits an atmosphere of confidence. It would be wise to focus on your particular level of your future, rather than on your past.

Learn to make use of your hidden potential.

We all know language is the means of communication, the more we try to use the more fluency we get. We should not try to take away the language of other people. The more you speak it is easier to communicate. If we replace the word language with money then we will see how we relate positively. Never think of taking away what they have, and be ready to help them, slowly everyone will prosper. Learn the art of winning over everyone. Find out the comprehension level of others and accordingly adjust it. Find out others nature and mould yourself with everyone you come across.

15

Establish Your Identity

To speak with you frankly, my father, H.K. Ojha was a deputy commandant of police in Mizoram. He was famous over there and we used to stay at Sivaji Tilla, Khatla, Aizawl, our neighbours were big officers like Kiran Bedi and many others.

Today there is no point in discussing all these; if I have to shine I cannot follow my father's footstep for that I need to work double. I can't carry his identity everywhere. I have to make my own identity and people should know me by my name Dilip Kumar Ojha.

If I keep thinking about my past, then it will be difficult for me to establish my own identity. Unless I stop giving importance to my father's identity, I will not be able to move forward and establish my identity. Everywhere I can't go and keep telling everyone that I am Ojha's son. And I know everything about Kiran Bedi, how good she is in lawn tennis. I had often seen her playing with her daughter. All these things will not help me. I will have to do something different that will set me apart. I have to come out from my father's shadow. There are many ways. Not of all of them well travelled, but they may be short cut to success. The new course may be difficult and tiring but if you follow whole heartedly, you can come out from others identity and get your own identity. This doesn't mean that I do not love them, I really do love them very much. I want to prove them that whatever support and guidance they have given me, has really helped me in making my own identity. Thank you very much once again to my loving father and mother.

You should know your strength and weakness. It will help you to select the direction, and to make a reputation for yourself. What is more important is to establish your identity. Not by seeking to distance yourself from your family but by learning from your family's strength, your mother and father will never be an obstacle. They will support you, and definitely guide you. There are endless things to learn from parents.

We all have hidden power within us but we do not always allow our self to use them.

16

Be Bold Enough to Handle Stress

Life is full of challenge. It has become a fitness challenge. If you want to survive you have to be bold enough to take decision. There is no place for timidity you will get more respect for your boldness. You have to practice boldness in every part of your life, and for that you need to practice on a fairly regular basis. Try to avoid leniency and compromising attitude your price tag should be high. Keep your mind cool no matter whatever stress arises at work and take bold step. You have to come out of your comfort zone and take bold steps even if there is a risk of failure. You have to change your perception and outdated ideas and untie the rope of your life which is holding you back and hiding the inner strength that you have. Try to be uncomfortable with being comfortable and be comfortable with being uncomfortable. This shows thatyou are taking a bold step.

Give a heavy shower of praise to your strength, and your strength will expand. While taking bold steps you should feel that your steps are positive, fulfilling and of cogent value. In this modern world, everyone has to deal with stress and pressure in different way.

It is full of misunderstanding, and less tolerance, you have to become that somebody to guide and force to take bold step at the time of stress. A bold move will make you larger than you are. You have to learn the art of audacity. If you take your steps with boldness then you can easily overcome the obstacle, the bold action that you take will magnify your strength. To be different you have to push you limit and never worry about perfection. It is natural to feel a little trepidation when we try to come out of the comfort zone, but do not keep it for tomorrow.

We all know that unless you drive your car. Your car is not going to move, however sophisticated it is.

I still remember the day, when I was taking class in F.T.I., ministry of labour at Jamshedpur. On my first day, after seeing my mature students, who were all engineers and had come to attend the class. I was gripped with fear, and had stammered a bit. My heart was thumping and my mouth was dry. I exerted my will power and braced myself with bold action and I made it and I took the class. I even remember, during the break some of them came to me and told me, that it was the best lecture they have ever heard... at that juncture I felt so good, but I would like to share the secret, it was all because of my boldness. Even you can do many things which might be holding you and your future, with your bold step.

17

Action Oriented

If you really want to be action oriented. You must be kind and helpful in nature. Try to develop positive vibes around you. Learn to be candid and take practical action to deal with problem. Wherever a reasonable amount of thinking is needed start making decision. Try to take on a tough and difficult path that others have tried and failed, you have to be an open minded person, must be open to change. Never be complacent, I mean never be satisfied with your knowledge and hard work. Be ready to accept new ideas, if your qualification is not good, then in that case you can depend on your experiences and relationship and persuade them to help you in taking the right decision. You have to be proactive and your decision should be based on value driven. To be action oriented you have to be internally controlled and must have a clear plan of your future and then just imagine yourself in your future, right now no need to take action. Everyday you just think of your plan and imagine but no need to take action.

After some time you will feel some-thing is compelling you to think about it and will push you in the same motion. This is the right time to take action. Each and every cell will prepare you to be action oriented and then you can take action without giving a second thought. Proactive people uses proactive language I can, I will, I believe etc.

A reactive person uses reactive language I can't, I have to, if only. Action oriented approaches are the most satisfying and rewarding. Action oriented people never prejudice others with their limited knowledge. You have to keep inaction at bay, and should not compromise with dead end. You must never give up, but always fight to create something new and for that you need to be decisive. Avoid procrastination and delaying. You must practice idealization in each area of your life, by stepping on the limitation, and by thinking that you are not deprived of anything. Another thing to be action oriented is be true to yourself, and mould yourself out of the clay in whatever form you want to see.

You can take corrective actions and make adjustment to improve your performance and weed out all negative thoughts.

You should check the purpose of your life and if you do not have, then first of all you cheek the purpose of your life and then you can easily tolerate emotional discomfort.

18

Decision

Half of the people are just happy with, whatever fate brings them, and are ready to accept it as their fortune or luck. Nowadays it has become very difficult to take decision, for that we have to fight with self, fight with close relatives, fight with the society and fight with the system. It is just a simple decision to make or break a life. We fail miserably to take the right decision. The decision making situations come fast and so frequently that we get deceived. At the time of taking decision we just take decision by mistake. We sometimes take fatal decision, and we abide by them.

We take crucial decision at some turning point of life and for which we suffer throughout our lives. It is better not to take any decision in a snap.

Just think that life rarely gives us another chance and to get the best out of it you have to take the right decision. Never get scrutinise your decision by other people. Just think of God, and by the grace of God you will be able to take the right decision.

The decision takes our life in a particular direction without us even realising.

You know yourself better than anybody else. At the time of taking decision, never follow the old sources and go for professional help. The best thing you can do is to rely on your own conscious thinking and try to approach it from different perspective. It will allow you to see your option clearly from outside. You should take the decision at your own pace and shouldn't be in a hurry, at times we have had the frustrating experiences of taking decision. It may be even nerve racking. Try to take decision solely for yourself, you can't live others life. You should take decision like a man of action and implement like a man of thought. Either you have to take decision or wait for the miracle to happen. Whenever you are too much excited or extremely upset, never take the decision. A pessimist sees difficulty in every decision where as an optimist sees the opportunity in every decision. If you make your decision more efficiently then you can manage such decision and will be able to deliver better result. There is no doubt that woman takes a better decision in life. They have the ability to take decision. No matter whether she is a housewife or a working woman.

We are so oblivious that all sorts of thought are preoccupied, and the decisions we make are often not even realizing its consequences. Before taking decision just think about, how this will affect you and others, would it hurt them, help them etc.

Try to find out your feelings at the time of taking decision, thousands of thought fluctuates in your mind, find out if it is a positive thought or a negative thought. Find out the pros and cons of every value based decision. In case you take a wrong decision no need to panic, it is a human tendency to make mistake, but what is more important is to find out fuel from the wrong decision.

19

Agony of Leaders

The extreme suffering failure can't be predicted. It may be because of his own fault. It may be due to bad decision or due to his ego. It will end up in destruction. The stigma of shame incurred by a cowardly submission can never be effaced. It will be clearly visible. You need to come out and resurface once again and face the situation from different angle. The drop of poison of inaction once enters the blood of a leader will be transmitted to his future activities which will again result in failure. It will undermine him and paralyse his inner strength. At this point of time resurgence is the need of the hour. Cowardly submission by a leader will not allow him to take new thought for himself and for others. Lack of knowledge is the sole cause of misfortune. It is neither calmly planned nor shrewdly defined and was not logically carried out. You are a million times bigger in the inside than you are on the outside. Try to find out the degree of your suffering compared to those experienced by others. You have to change your perspective and regain your self-confidence. The greatest acid test of courage on earth is to bear defeat without losing heart. The next time you crash, pick yourself up, dust yourself off, shake off the cobweb,fix what went wrong. By doing this you can defeat your agony. Most of the time the problem comes from the mind rather than outer circumstance. All the problems are manmade. If you are facing issues then try to resolve issues in a timely manner and do it in a way that inspires people to do their best. In case your subordinate makes a blunder mistake, and if you shout at him for the mistake, that means you are destroying his self respect and yours. You should give them full freedom with whatever way he is comfortable with. It you have some ideas, and you are not using it, in that case you should feel free to give it to your subordinate, and allow them to play with your ideas. If you take the decision beyond your ken then you will have to face the music. If you want to come out from the agony, the decision you take should be based on value driven and must be credible.

To overcome the suffering you have undergone, the best thing is roll your sleeves and create a vision. Lack of vision will bring you down to the ground level. You have to develop an insatiable curiosity for great ideas, and must have a desire to learn and get some training in delegation skill.

20

Stop Comparision Blue and Trust Yourself

They sneak up on you without warning. The more and more you compare, you will always feel less adequate and you will become inferior.

Just remind yourself of your talent and the special potential which you have. You should be internally controlled. Everything can't be compared, but it's natural we start comparing the moment we see two different things. Just give a pat to yourself and stop comparing. Learn to nurture yourself. Just trust yourself, your instincts, intuition which are the tools of our life. You have all the answers inside you, the more you trust yourself, the easier your life will flow and will experience more joy, satisfaction and fulfilment. Sometimes comparing may help, it depends on how you are taking the comparison, if you use it to reinforce an unrealistic self image, then it is not good you will become inferior, and will take you no-where. Just remember you are what you are, if you have ever been an object of comparison, then you wouldn't feel like recalling it with fondness, and if you do then you wouldn't be able to come out of the vortex.

To share with you frankly, when I compare my first manuscript of my first book with other books, sometimes I feel that. I don't measure up with other books. I know my strength and my true value of the book, since then I have stopped comparing. Just count your blessing, and stop the habit of comparing. The more you ask feedback from others about your work, no doubt you will get, but you shouldn't be too willing to change in order to please. You inculcate a habit of trusting yourself or else you will not be able make your own choice. I am not telling you to stop listening to feedback. Feedback is important for the development, right now I mean to say if you do not take feedback then you will work harder, and will not mould yourself according to the suggestion. It is difficult to find out positive feedback or negative feedback.

If you are really looking for somebody whom you can trust, then you have to become that somebody to be trusted. Try to be mercurial, at times mercurial temperament may not be good. It will be difficult to predict your movement your thought and your steps. Your mood will keep changing.

On the other hand if you see they are quick witted, animated, lively. You should not be wet blanket and shouldn't kill the joy of others. Trust yourself and try to be phlegmtic, and take your steps in a way you are willing to step, you shouldn't get bounded by others. Cowardly submission to anyone is not going to help you to build your trust. Lily livered person has no place. You have to fight for your inner strength, and trust your inner instinct. You must renew the vital energy of yourself and inspire it once more with a resolute determination to come back from the comparison blue. You need to pluck up sufficient courage and energy.

- If you nurture the seed of inferiority it will act as a drop of poison and once it get noticeable. Then it will aggravate on all your future decision. If you just act as a wind bag, then you may become an object of derision these type of people will fabricate thousands of ground for excuses, but in no way admit, he himself is the chief cause of the failure. Just trust yourself and put your best foot forward to avoid the object of subordinate raillery.

- Believe in yourself and make people listen to you.
- Once you have set a goal or a vision you must not keep changing for anything or for anyone.
- You must rely on yourself to carry out your plan.
- You must make others hollow in front of you.
- You must set a realistic goal .
- You must have a good audacity.
- You must be good at getting people to follow you.
- You cannot be a strong minded person if you are not secure with yourself.

21

Transform Your Ways

Everyone
juncture You
lust, self-
corrupt th
you need
God. You
SHIRDI
is there
difficulties
will feel,
you. We
hardly have
personal
days and
getting on
blessing.

All
If you want

21

Transform Your Ways

Everyone of us has bad habits and as well as good habits. At this juncture you have to stop all your bad habits. It can be your lust, self-centeredness or any sin. Just put off you negative and corrupt thinking. You have to practice tough love, and for that you need to have a constant discipline, start praying to your God. You need to re-surrender to God. If you get time go to SHIRDI, VAISNODEVI etc. and see the changes yourself. He is there to handle your problem, to come out from your difficulties and problem. Please stop all your had habits.You will feel, he is there every time to hold your finger and guide you. We are so inundated in our modern mundane life, that we hardly have time to think of God. I am telling you from my personal experience, I really had lots of bad habit in my school days and college life. Now I have stopped and as a result, I am getting on smoothly in my life. I have started counting my blessing. Just have faith in God, and believe him everywhere.

All big people have inculcated a habit of visiting temple. If you want to come up, then you must have belief in God and stop from today itself all those bad habits which is holding you, and is not allowing you to see the bright side of your future. Just trust him, he will make your path straight. You will not get anything from anyone, except from your LORD.

22

Aspire Big

Sometimes it depends on your family and the environment where you stay, tend to make an aspiration too small. No doubt it is difficult to come out of the vortex, but if you have calibre then why should you live a life of poverty, millions of people have accepted whatever fate has given them. They are neither comfortable nor bothered to change their life style.

The best part is, you should visualize how great your life will be, if you change, and how horrible, it will be if you keep going the way you are going. When the time will come to go to graveyard, either you will feel happy or extremely sad for many things that you could have done. Do you want people to remember you after your death. Then you have to make an identity of your own. Expand the depth of your mind and never think about an average life. Think big. But that should be your by product. You need to be different and must judge yourself by your own standard and not by the outside world. The average is just what everyone else is doing, but you should have a will to be different, if you have to come out from your comfort zone. Suppose you are playing football and you are spending too much time defending in your own zone, how are you going to make a goal on the other hand.

Never multitask yourself you have to sweat out extra, and a lot of concentration and effort is needed to do any task. Suppose you are making rice in a cooker and after every 5 minutes there is a problem in your gas stove. Then in that case it will be more time consuming to get your rice ready. If you get distracted even for 5 minutes, it takes some time to come back once again and start the work. If you keep changing your aspiration as you come across obstacle or any problems, you are not going to live your true life. Just take action, forget about the obstacle it will come in life anyway, it is a part and parcel of our life you can't change the course. Learn to confront it and step on your obstacle and get ahead in your life.

Whenever you talk with your friends try to select a good word that has a pack of punch. So that you do not have to worry about any extra word to carry the message. You are hesitating to flaunt off your ideas but at least you should take action and implement it. Never talk about trivial matter, talk about prosperity. Think about expansion, and never hang out with petty thinkers. It is better to lose an argument rather than your friends. Think big and focus on important things. Sometimes it so happens that when we get an opportunity to aspire, at times, we refuse and the reason which we give are as clear as mud. Like, I know nothing about the responsibility, sometimes we even say that I do not want to allow myself to be forced, into anything.

These are the profound mistakes we make when the blessing comes in disguise. The one who is lucky may take the challenge and aspire big, then at that time you will stand dumbfounded. You have to become more independent. Then you will be able to understand the inner cause of success. Have you ever thought of doing something different and if you feel that you have no initiative, in that case you need a catalyst which can help you in sparking your initiative to do something different. Try to inculcate a will to do it and learn to disengage your attention from objects of distraction. You must never live at the mercy of strong emotion like anger, depression and anxiety. When you keep thinking about your goal, and focus on it, even the outside world will be in your favour. Never send a negative or failure signal to yourself . Always expect a successful outcome of your work. Aspire big and never allow any negative thought to enter. Keep a list of thought changer and replace it at once. You shouldn't feel hollow inside, and if you are feeling hollow, then learn to give respect and love to yourself, always aspire big and start hoping for it.You should have a vision for it or else you will never be able to aspire big. Learn to nurture the seed of hope. The bigger your seed of hope is the more you will receive. The unknown is little bit tripidated, and many people resist change because it is more comforting in the comfort zone.

23

Follow The Cue

Learn something from all successful people, how do they interact and with whom do they interact. Try to make friends with people having the same interest you should look at competency never talk about others salary, cost of house, or car and never be a story teller. Try to avoid being a proclaimed back bencher. Learn to transfer ideas into words, and connect your past learning with you present. Remember to begin with an end in mind. You need to figure out what that goal is.

Everything is created twice there is a mental creation and then a physical creation. Suppose you have to construct a house, you will not just start the work. First you will visit the architecture and get the blue print, and then you will visualize the whole house with your family. The extent to which you begin with the end in mind determines your chances of success. For all these you need the power of imagination. You must have a clear understanding of your life. Only understanding alone will not make it happen. For that you have to take action and that's what you have to learn from the successful people. Enjoy each and every moment of your life, without fear and regret. Just fight for your life and for your work and let others know how much it means to you. Never get disappointed when you come across any obstacle, learn something from the failure, find out fuel from the failure and move on gracefully. Take out your precious time and learn to renew your relationship with your friend you love, it will refresh your mind.

Give quality time to your children and your family. Try to focus on the most important work and give time to it, and the other small works will get managed. You can act as a catalyst in finding out the strength in them. Follow the recipes of the successful people, never try to be an egoist, learn to listen, it might help you in gaining your respect and relationship. Never get discouraged quickly we all want result fast and in an easy way never allow to vaporise your dream, stay connected with it all times. Never turn a blind eye to your dream and never give up. Always accept your mistake as a stepping stone, and try to be broadminded by reading books and sharing knowledge.

24

You will become Strong in An Isolation

At times you feel more pleased, when you are in a group and following a common line in action, and mutually depending on each other. You feel stronger in this group, but you check it pragmatically, then you will know that it is better to have one goal for one person. If you want to be different, you make your goal and work on it. Whatever big things that you do show that there was a desire for it and was getting nourished slowly within your heart.

The moment you get success, and if you are in a group, then your friends start following and will be in a little bit hurry to find another way which will lead them to the same goal, they may even join you when you are becoming the centre of attraction.

Then your other friend who were in a group will also sniff and reach to your level. It should never be forgotten that, good ideas never comes out in a group. All success whatever have been made are the result of sincere and honest hardworking of an individual, at the time of credit everyone joins to take the credit.

Suppose you have a sparking idea, but the friend with whom you share your idea is a duffer. Your strength will come down by joining with a duffer. If you leave your ideas to be controlled by duffer, then your act will get paralysed. The point is when you are alone, you will apply yourself more efficiently and you can rely on it but when you are in a group.

Your ideas will be scrutinize by other people who may not be ready to accept and may repudiate his masterpiece suggestion. When you are in a group your self-esteem will not grow, and may have problem in your personal growth. When you are in a group, everything will remain good, as long as there is no change, but the moment any one from your group comes up with an idea, then your relationship with your friend may go down when you are in a group, you will feel other people as more capable and responsible to deal in life. Never suppress your freedom of thought, and see things free from other people's ideas, and must build your own understanding in order to become strong. Your sincere effort will get recognised, and your talent will be exposed. If you are too much dependent then you will not be able to recognise the blessing that you have.

No doubt you are strong but when you are left alone, you get more strength to experiment yourself without getting dominated by others. You will be able to assimilate your hidden energy; which will help you in your personal growth. The feeling that nobody is behind you to guide or to stop you from playing with your ideas, will help you in motivating you to be strong enough to handle the situation. It doesn't mean you can't survive in a group or you shouldn't take the help of your group. It will definitely help you, but if you will learn to handle stress yourself that will be much better for you in your upcoming life. You have to set a benchmark for yourself. If you will share your problems with others, at times they will make fun of you and you may become an object of mockery. Try to learn something from the individuals who have excelled in their life.

Do not misunderstand that I am forcing you to live alone what I mean to say is when you are alone it will force you to be strong and teach you to be more responsible. You can deal with yourself where as when you are in a group, you may mimic others opinion and will never be self reliant.

Just take all the steps you can when you are alone and practice tough love with your life and in a disciplined way you will see your success coming in disguise, and you can move forward with it. It is up to you, just do what is in your heart. Always remember you are more strong when you are alone. You can face all sorts of difficulties with your inner power which will become double when you have to face yourself.

25

Secret of Success

You must have a will to change, and if you are not comfortable with the changes, then you will end up heading nowhere. Come out of the comfort zone, and accept change with your hidden strength. The world is not going to change, you have to face the reality and act accordingly. Then you will definitely win. Allow your subordinate the freedom to think and implement, and you do not have to keep tab on their work. Take out your precious time to emphasize new ideas and be open to ideas from anywhere. Learn to be energetic and vibrant and try to meet aggressive targets. As you think, so shall you be. So flush out all old, tired, worn out thoughts, fill your mind with fresh, new creative thought.

If you want to have a king Midas touch then you have to touch your work with an optimistic attitude. Allow new thoughts to come and let it displace the old thought which might be the main cause of your failure. If you really want to know the secret of success, then first of all you must have a good idea, must have faith in it, and have to take action on it by visualizing it. Never allow negative thought of defeat to come into your mind.

Your visualization combined with prayer and faith will definitely actualize achievement. Never keep distance from God, Just visualize, as if he is holding your hand and showing you the right track. When you have the support of God, then why should you allow negative thought to dominate.

Try to do that type of work where you can give your whole heart with love then you see the limit of happiness. Select an environment where you can have fun and make a difference, just learn to love the work you do. Many people have a feeling that most of the jobs are boring where as some people have a feeling that most of the jobs can be performed with energy and enthusiasm.

There is always a choice about the way you handle your work even if there is no tolerance in the work.You always have a choice about the attitude you bring to your work. If you take your work with casual attitude, then you will have a bad day. If you take your work whole heartedly, with a playful, and cheerful attitude then you will have a great day. The reason you were born was to leave your own identity in the world and to become famous rather than to accept the death bed living ordinarily. The bitter truth of life is everyone has hidden talent which has never been used and exploited and you have lots of inner strength which you have never utilised. You must have seen sometimes the back benchers start making noise or disturb the class whenever a weak teacher enters the class, but the moment the principal enters you will find a pin drop silence in the class, because he makes them stand on a bench, or makes them raise their hands or rap them on the knuckles. This shows how they respond. It is in your hand to choose a choice in order to build self control and courage. No one will come and offer you idea everyday, it is you who have to choose your attitude, and the way you respond everyday and choose it well. You are the only one who can make or spoil your life. There is no point in blaming others.

Whenever you take decision, do not worry about perfect decision or the best decision, what you need at this juncture is to take a better decision. If your mind is full of doubt then good decision can't get through. You should prioritise everything and do what you need to do first, then worry about what you want to do. If you think honestly, you will see yourself that it takes less time to make a better decision but more time consuming to correct a poor decision. You should be internally controlled and must be aware of the options coming in disguise to you. Average people feel that if somebody at their level or below goes an inch upwards, they would be going a few inches down. If you want to come up in your life, you have to avoid backbiting, gossiping, lying, and dumping one's work load on to others. You shouldn't feel insecure when you are in a group of bright person. Learn something from them.

If you can sense and are aware of situations, then you can avoid unpleasantness before it gets build up, even if you have become an object of fun, you shouldn't think of recriminating or retaliating. Always belief yourself that you can do it, you have to find the belief that will support your wish and get you where you want to go. The secret of all successful people is, they think in terms of possibilities, and never bother about negative feedback they get from their environment. Learn painful lessons, mend fences and take a good look at new possibilities, suppose you have tried and have failed then accept it as a learning experience and use it what you have learned and try something else.

Everyone has had a frustrating experience of many things that didn't work out. You should accept it as a learning experience and try it again or try something else. Many people keep procrastinating their work due to fear of failure, which is the greatest limitation. Try to build a good rapport among your friends, learn to respect them rather than manipulating them.

Keep tuning yourself and recalling your actions, to make sure you must develop a will, practice saying how can I do it, if you will say how can I do it, your mind will start working and if you say I can't do it, your mind will stop working. Another thing is, if you say you can do it, you open up the pathways that can provide you with the resource of achievement and if you say you can't do it, you shut down all the pathways that can make it happen.

Everyone has a different perspective. Some people have a habit of selecting a pathway by excluding other path ways, whereas some people have a habit of creating a new pathway.

Some people have a habit of looking for different approaches. Whereas some people have a habit of generating new approaches. Some people have a habit of moving in the direction of comfort zone. Some people have a habit of coming out from a comfort zone and looking for a challenging zone. Some people just follow the path others have left behind, where as some people do not give up, and they look for new path, and take risk.

Some people always worry about mistake where as some people do not mind on being wrong on the way to a solution.

26

The Art of Communication

The common mistake we make is, we talk but never listen. Communication should be reciprocal. Otherwise it becomes a monotonous lecture. Everyone should get a chance to speak. You can paraphrase the statement and let them repeat. When you speak, you should be candid and never use vulgar language. At the time of speaking, just think a bit and then speak in case you need to apologise, you shouldn't hesitate otherwise communication will deteriorate. Do not go after contentious issue and never try to offer unsolicited advice. Maintain eye contact and find areas of common interest.

Try to avoid frequent correction when you speak, and focus on your intonation, movement of your voice. You should know when to raise your voice and when to bring down. If you will make mockery of others religion, he or she may feel compelled to go against you no matter whether you are talking with a broadminded or narrow minded people nobody will encourage you. You must steer clear of this topic. You should avoid off colour topics and risqué jokes, when you communicate, and must never raise this type of topics.

Never bother about personal affairs of others, it is impolite and indecent. It is better not to narrate your dull events of your life. Keep your general awareness up to date, and never try to bore others with your emotional topics.

You should be articulate; I mean you should express your thoughts clearly and must find out the comprehension level and try to use simpler words. There shouldn't be any misunderstanding or else it will mar your communication, the moment you communicate remember it must focus on the solution rather than focusing on the problems. You should be trustworthy and never try to mislead others. It is much more than just exchanging information.

Never try to become centre of attraction by dominating others. You must never be so engrossed in your words that you seldom give attention to others. In a group you have to check that you do not lose track of what you are saying. If you wish others to respect your words, you have to develop consideration and respect. You will help yourself in creating a new self confidence, and will become energetic and vibrant in your communication.When all thinks alike, hardly any one is thinking.

Suppose you are planning to do something and suddenly you hit a plan of taking opinions of your friends, suppose if all of them come up with the same idea, in that case you have to be careful. I mean when all thinks alike, no one thinks very much. You should encourage diverse opinion, and dynamic new ideas, and if you will discourage diverse opinion and dynamic new ideas, then it will curb the stream of ideas that give birth to new ideas. The only ways to eliminate like thinking is to uncover the fact that it is no longer dangerous to disagree with others opinion. You should feel free to repudiate others opinion, theory or statement especially when you disapprove of it.

If you feel that an attempt is made to have a binding force on you and make you accept the same thought you can repudiate your friendship. When you are in a group, you should encourage everyone to think differently. Sometimes the provocation is supplied by the ideas of others. At times ideas from outside one's mind, can serve to stimulate one's own ideas. Sometimes it so happens that others output becomes someone's input. Ideas which seems trivial to one person may combine with others ideas and might work out for somebody else. No idea is big or small. So long it keeps the wheel of new ideas generating. If everyone nods in agreement, remember they are trying to please you. They just try to jump on the bandwagon if it is getting familiar or popular.

Most people take the safe route they do not want to be different. If you do something different, everyone would like to keep tab on you and they will check you out.

27

God is Inside You

Remember before doing any illegal things make sure that God is not watching you which is not possible. We all know God is inside us. You can make fool of everyone but you can't fool him, he is with us every-time. You will get more strength and support if you will follow his guide lines. Have faith in him no matter how huge may be the problem. Why do we fear? When he is here he has no beginning... he has no end. To write with you frankly even I was an atheist. I didn't believe in God, now time has changed. I love him, and have got full strength in me to handle all stress. I request you everyone, to take out your precious time and just visit once. You will get change, from all angles, you have to stop all bad things in which you were comfortable, now come out from the comfort zone and try to live a life of his wishes never try to cheat anyone, remember he is watching you. Once you start getting this feeling that means you are following the true path of success. He will definitely help everyone of us, who is willing to take out their precious time for him; when we cannot love man whom we can see then how can we think of God whom we cannot see.

28

Too Much Perfection can be an Obstacle

Some people have a habit of expecting only the best and have an insatiable curiosity for doing perfectly. Sometimes you find this type of person as your co-worker or managers.

They never accept anything imperfect, and keep looking for flaws in their employees work. It results in delay and overshooting deadlines. They are more time consuming in their work.

Too much perfection leads to self-destruction and will directly blightened the career of yourself and your co-workers. Accept the fact that no one is perfect and infalliable.

Never lament on your mistake too much regret is also a blunder. You should delegate your work, and have trust in others. Learn to accept imperfectness, that one day lead to perfection.

You can get clarity of your work by breaking the work into a manageable chunk. If you get bogged down, then take a break. Never be in a hurry to complete your work.

- Forgive
- Be open
- Have fun
- Self check
- Focus
- Delegate
- Prioritise
- Burning desire
- One thing at a time
- A conscious decision
- Retrospect your goal
- Do not portray in negative light.

You have a choice to get back after temporary setbacks. Just have to change your attitude and see the difference yourself. Just put your dreams on papers, it will get locked in your memory. If you do not see perfection, set aside and relax and then raise the bar and analyse the areas that you need to change. Explore what is important. Stick to the task, even if you are uncomfortable, encouragement and love to your co-workers are the contagious qualities that can change the mind of imperfectionist. Working on multiple tasks at a time can lead to overload that will play havoc with your attention.

Going back to single tasking emerges as the best option as you can start concentrating solely on one task until it gets done.

Everyone would like you to finish the work perfectly. Just eliminate the word perfection, and go ahead with your work seriously. You may be surprised to realise the amount of time that is wasted in constantly reviewing, in sorting through your mail.

The result is that we lose attention frequently and end up just wasting time as we are unable to concentrate, and get little time for analysis and corrections. When we run after perfection the end product may deviate.

30

29

Allow to Reinforce These Words

1. Love your job but don't love your company because you may not know when your company stops loving you.
   ————*Dr. Abdul Kalam*

2. What is the secret of success...?
   ——*Right decisions*

   How do you make right decisions?
   ——Experience

   How do you get experience?
   ——- *Wrong decisions*

   Dr. Abdul Kalam

3. Behind every successful man, there is an untold pain in his heart.
   ——-*Bill Jacobs*

4. Without your involvement you can't succeed. With your involvement you can't fail
   Dr. Abdul Kalam

5. You are not responsible for what people think about you. But you are responsible for what you give them to think about you.

   ———-*Stanley Ferrard*

6. Don't make promise when you are in Joy...

   Don't reply when you are sad....

   Don't take decisions when you are angry.

   Think twice, Act wise

7. Effort-fully releases its reward only when a person refuses to quit.

30

Everyone is in a Hurry

It doesn't happen overnight there is a gap between everything to get materialize. We have no patience for anything.

Once we are on the road and behind the wheels, we are in a hurry to reach our destination; jumping signals, cutting lanes, over speeding, overtaking, honking, road rage, getting licences on the sly. It's all considered normal. How impatient and rash we are. Whenever we stop at a traffic signal, we leave no room for the other vehicle to reverse. We have made our life so fast and tense. If you want to achieve in life, there is no point to be in a hurry. Act in a moment thoughtfully according to the situation, and see the changes in your life.

Parents set example. They are also guilty of transferring the same to the next generation. Sometimes, parents also bow under the usual pressure. They are also in a hurry to see their son's name in the merit list.

Sometimes they nag and pressurise their children, taking away their freedom to decide. Even at work, there would be a tendency to grumble and expect the world to suit your mood.

We practically bully the other drivers to make way for us. We are on our path of destruction by following the negligent and rash pace.

Everywhere you see road rage, which shows the reflection of the prevalence.

There is a process for everything, no need to be in a hurry.

31

Gap in Our Education

Our education system is not producing enough people with the essential soft skills, communication skills, business etiquette and cultural sensitivity are the key drivers of career growth and success rather than a high degree of technical skills.

To capitalise fully on the opportunity, we need to go for high quality education. Soft skills have become very important and has enough power to make or break your career.

Soft skills can help you to deal with people. Even today many companies keep away from providing training on soft skills. If you take an honest look 'soft skills have graduated from a 'nice to have' category to the must-have' category. Let us fill this gap. Soft skills play a vital role for professional success. It cannot be denied in this age of information. Awareness is the first step in building up your soft skills. Learn to interact more. Be creative and hone your innovative and creative skills.

Nowadays recruiters are jumping on the soft skill bandwagon. It has become extremely important to have both, soft skills and technical skills.

With your soft skill, you can excel as a leader. It will be easy for you to delegate, and motivate. It will help your attitude to be positive and upbeat. I mean you will feel more cheerful and happy.

It will be easy for you to handle complex decision, and will also help you to manage yourself and others.

Soft skill is connected with everything. Soft skill will put people in a position to innovate, and will also help you to make basic business decision. Sometimes it so happens that because of poor outcome the relationship is at stake. Soft skills will help you to put teams in a great position to innovate.

Etiquette can be embellished by small talk and humour. It depends on language and culture. It cannot be changed in a day or two. It is a slow process.

32

Personal Branding

Personal branding is a powerful way of communicating the unique promise.

Personal

Understand your true self, limitation and strength. Remember you are an original, there is no one else like you, take some time to discover your strength and limitation.

Perception:

Must be aware of how you communicate yourself with those around, find out your attributes and how others perceive you.

Position:

Try to target your business audience and job competitors. How will you stand out without knowing whom you are standing among.

When people see your name or face consistently over a period of time they assume that you have something special.

Performance

Establish yourself as an expert in your field. Expertise can bring you increased recognition. You can position yourself in the hearts and minds of others.

Promoting

You are good but if no one knows about you then you will not go ahead. Nothing in marketing is more powerful than a promotion tool called word of mouth.

Planning

Make an appointment with yourself at least twice a month. You have to re-evaluate and obtain honest and helpful feedback.

It is easy to be happy when things are sailing smoothly, but during crisis it is rather difficult to maintain a happy and healthy state of mind. You can be happy even in tough times, if you focus with your determination. During economic downturn the need of the hour is the best of individuals and individuals give the best only when they are happy.

Effort should be duly awarded and shouldn't be frowned as long as output is honest. Occasional motivation can keep up the happiness level. Avoid accepting any kind of work. Never put in airs. You should never wear a mask on your personality. Never try to betray and add fuel in office politics.

33

Global Recession

During the time of global recession there is a fear about job and financial security. Their morale and confidence is on the downward slide. With no clear sign of things to come, you have to become proactive.

Control Emotion

It is easy to blame your boss, economy and your bad luck for all your troubles. It is not going to help you and your problem. Remove all your clutters and stop your needless worries. You have to stay informed about the market. You have to keep an eye open for opportunities. Steer clear of office politics, and stop the blame game. Don't allow conflict to lead towards resentment. Learn to read between the lines and become more conscious.

Choose your words carefully and avoid those statements which can eventually lead to an argument.

Consolidate Position

Find out organisation need and align your priorities with the organisation, get involved in project, give your best and work hard, and try to be responsive. Upgrade your skills, and keep abreast of information.

Team

Communicate effectively, try to keep relationship, always pay attention to instruction. Ask for help where you need it. Help others when they need.

Prepare for Future

Look for alternative career and check the status of other industries in between attend a few interviews. Don't fall a prey to the vagaries of an unsteady economy.

34

Carve Your Future by Your Effort

Nobody is going to do you a favour. It is you who have to come up in life and take action. Stop making false excuses. It is not going to help you in anyway. Success is directly proportional to your effort. Don't just sit on your hands and wait for the miracle to happen. There is no shortcut, no miracle will take place. It is you who has to take your first step, and you are responsible for your life. You should never say 'No' to any type of responsibility. Take it as a challenge. Never try to cover up failure with your air bag of excuses.

Just go ahead, and face the entire obstacle. You shouldn't quit your effort. Never give up your effort. Effort alone will help you. Allow action to dominate. Unless you take action, nothing is going to change. If you keep making false excuses, or try to hide yourself from taking action, then one day you will regret. Action is the reflection of your will power. You have to get your act together. If you are not action oriented, then you will lag behind in the race of the world. We eat food everyday to get energy, there is no doubt about it. In the same way read this book and reinforce it and get refreshed instantly with life changing thought. It will help you to participate in the long race of the world. The bitter truth for many of us for not getting what we want is, we give time for trifle things. At least think about the benefit which your children will get at the cost of your action. You will get more respect before and after. One small failure doesn't end your life. Get up and dust off, then move ahead stepping on the obstacle with your clear vision in your mind. Unless you sweat out nothing will change. Ideas will remain in the book. Try to give it a primary importance. If you want to see a change in your life, then this book will act as a curtain raiser in your life.

We people have a habit of taking trifle things to our heart. If someone doesn't wish you, remember do not take it to your heart.

- If someone doesn't inform you, remember don't take it to your heart.
- Suppose you have become an object of derision, remember don't take it to your heart.
- You didn't get promotion on time, remember do not take it to your heart.
- No one invites you for party, remember don't take it to your heart.
- If you fail once, remember don't take it to your heart.

Do not live your life with hate in your heart, you will end up hurting yourself more than the people you hate. Learn to forgive yourself, move on, and try to do better next time. Never refuse to lower your standard to accommodate those who refuses to raise theirs.